Lili at Ballet

Rachel Isadora

PaperStar

The Putnam & Grosset Group

Copyright © 1993 by Rachel Isadora
All rights reserved. This book, or parts thereof, may not be
reproduced in any form without permission in writing from the publisher.
A PaperStar Book, published in 1996 by The Putnam & Grosset Group,
200 Madison Avenue, New York, NY 10016.
PaperStar Books and the PaperStar logo are trademarks of
The Putnam Berkley Group, Inc. Originally published in 1993 by
G. P. Putnam's Sons, New York. Published simultaneously in Canada.
Printed in the United States of America
Library of Congress Cataloging-in-Publication Data
Isadora, Rachel.
Lili at ballet / written and illustrated by Rachel Isadora.
p.   cm.
Summary: Lili dreams of becoming a ballerina and goes to her
ballet lessons four afternoons a week.
[1. Ballet dancing—Fiction.]   I. Title.
PZ7.1763Li   1993   [E]—dc20   CIP   AC
ISBN 0-698-11408-6
1   3   5   7   9   10   8   6   4   2

For Gillian

This is Lili. She dreams of becoming a ballerina. Sometimes she
dances at home with her cat, Pandora.

When Lili saw the ballet *Giselle* with her dance class, she wanted to practice even harder. She knows there will be many years of hard work ahead before she can join a ballet company.

long-sleeved leotard

sleeveless leotard

tights

short practice tutu

tutu with bodice

Lili has ballet lessons four afternoons a week. Everyone wears clothes made just for dancing. Lili tries on a long practice tutu.

pointe
shoes

ballet
slippers

footless
tights

socks

T-shirt

leg
warmers

She thinks about being the flower fairy in the school performance at the end of the year.

Students get ready for class in the dressing rooms. They change into leotards and tights. Some put up their hair. Others work on their homework or sew elastic on their ballet slippers.

Lili likes dancing to classical music played on the piano. The mirrors show the students how their steps look. They hold onto the barre for balance.

bending forward
to stretch back
and legs

lunging forward
to arch back
and stretch legs

stretching on the floor
to turn out the hips
and arch the back

Students do warm-up stretches and bends before class. These exercises make their muscles limber.

feet touching,
knees turned out
to turn out the legs

backbend to stretch
back and arms

side split to stretch legs
and back and turn out the legs

Here is Lili's teacher, Madame Popova. The first exercise begins
at the barre. Madame Popova tells Nanette to pull in her tummy
and reminds the class to turn out their feet.

grand pas de chat
développé

jeté

These are some of the ballet steps. Ballet began in France about
300 years ago, and the steps are still called by their French names.

passé
en pointe

changement
en l'air

attitude

arabesque

first position

second position

After the barre work is finished, the students move to the center of the floor. They practice the five classical positions. Now they must balance on their own.

third position   fourth position   fifth position

During the last part of class, Madame Popova asks the students to combine steps and dance across the floor. These are called *combinations*. The students leap and turn, using the whole studio space. Lili likes this part of class the best.

Lili has seen ballerinas on stage dance on their toes, or *sur les pointes*. When she is older and her feet are stronger, she will begin practicing *en pointe*, too.

Girls begin to go en pointe around the age of eleven. They wear their pointe shoes for a few minutes at the end of their ballet class. As their bones and muscles strengthen they will wear their pointe shoes for longer periods of time and do more difficult steps.

Shank: a stiff support for the arch in the sole of the shoe

Drawstring tightens the shoe around the foot.

Vamp: the upper part of the front of the shoe

Box: the entire front of the shoe, most of which is stiff

Satin ribbons tie around the ankle for support.

Rosin box:
rosin is used
to prevent
slipping

Most students wear
pink satin pointe
shoes for class.

Pointe shoes are
sometimes dyed different
colors to match the
ballerina's costumes.

"stag" jeté

croisé derrière

There is also a special class just for boys. They practice jumping high and turning fast.

pas de poisson

grand pas de chat
développé

Lili can't wait until she's old enough for the *variations* class. There she'll learn roles from different ballets and perform them in recital. Lili's class has been practicing to be flowers in their student performance.

Candy Cane from
"The Nutcracker"

The White Cat and
Puss in Boots
from "The Sleeping Beauty"

Odette from
"Swan Lake"

Albrecht and Giselle
from "Giselle"

Firebird from
"The Firebird"

Petroushka from
"Petroushka"

When the night of the school performance arrives, Lili dances the part of the flower fairy. She waves her wand and the flowers begin to dance.

Backstage, after the performance, Lili still feels like the flower fairy.
She waves her wand, smiles, and makes a secret wish.